Grumpy Cat®

YAWN!

A Grumpy Cat Bedtime Story

By **Steve Foxe** • Illustrated by **Steph Laberis**

🦌 A GOLDEN BOOK • NEW YORK

grumpycats.com
rhcbooks.com
Educators and librarians, for a variety of teaching tools, visit us at RHTeachersLibrarians.com
ISBN 978-1-5247-2055-1 (trade)—ISBN 978-1-5247-2056-8 (ebook)
Printed in the United States of America
10 9 8 7 6 5 4 3 2 1

"**G**rumpy Cat, it's almost bedtime!
It's our last chance to play today!"

"I prefer to sleep one hour....
every hour."

"A glass of milk will make you sleepy, Grumpy Cat."

"This milk reminds me of my mood: sour."

"Better wash up before bed!"

"Rub-a-dub-dub, get me out of this tub."

"Let's wear matching pajamas tonight."

"I've got the perfect prickly
pair in mind."

"Grumpy Cat, will you read me a bedtime story?"

"Pretty please,
Grumpy Cat?
This one's my favorite."

"Let's skip to the best part...."

"And they all lived grumpily
ever after. The end."

"I think I need my night-light after that gloomy story, Grumpy Cat."

"I prefer the darkness."

"Before we fall asleep, will you please
tuck me in, Grumpy Cat?"

"You've already tuckered me out."

"Good night, Grumpy Cat."

"Good riddance."